MOPSWORTH CUSTARD - ZOMBIE INVASION OF EARTH

Alastair MacDonald

Cover design by: Alastair MacDonald
Library of Congress Control Number: 2018675309
Printed in the United States of America

This book is dedicated my friends, their children
and everyone who loves to eat custard.

CONTENTS

CHAPTER ONE

Ambassador Murray sits at his desk drinking a chilled glass of Gragg juice. It is a specialty of Mars and as Mars's Ambassador to Earth he has the power and authority to request weekly deliveries of Gragg juice from his home planet of Mars. Gragg juice is made from the milk of a Gragg, which is like a camel, but it has three humps. The Gragg juice is mixed with juice squeezed from an old sweaty sock. To serve the drink it is decorated with an old sock draped over the top of the glass and a stripy straw.

To Ambassador Murray it looked perfect.

To explain, Murray The Martian is Mars's first Ambassador to Earth. He was made Ambassador after Earth won the Intergalactic Games with a surprise late entry team. Murray's hope is that he can stay in this job until the next Intergalactic Games. The Intergalactic Games are held every 150 years, so this means Murray has crossed all his toes, all fourteen of them to wish himself luck. Martians live for a thousand years, so this is easily possible, as long as he does not make a big mess out of things.

The location of the Mars Embassy is in a small town in Yorkshire, in the UK, called Mopsworth. Why did Mars choose Mopsworth you may ask yourself? The answer is simple, Mopsworth is the home to the world famous Mopsworth Custard Mine.

The Mopsworth Custard Company produces fresh dairy free custard that comes from deep underground. No one knows where it comes from, but no one cares because all the children in the world love custard. It just keeps filling up the old coal mine. It was discovered by a miner called Bert Twiglet when he was digging for coal with his pickaxe. He is the world's first Custard hero. He has even been knighted by the Queen of England for his discovery. He is now called Lord Twiglet of Mopsworth.

Murray's best friends are Benjy and Elicia Twiglet. Their father is Lord Twiglet of Mopsworth. Benjy and Elicia Twiglet helped save Mopsworth from evil Russian oligarch Igor Bagsofmoneyov and keeps Mopsworth Custard for all the children in the world. Murray met Benjy and Elicia at NASA where they made food for the first manned space mission to Mars. The rest is history.

So every day the Mopsworth Custard Company sends fresh Mopsworth Custard out in large road tankers, big barrels and bottles so that it can be sold all over the world. Mopsworth Custard is responsible for supplying fresh custard to all the world's children and even to the Martian children on Mars.

Therefore, since the discovery of custard under the town of Mopsworth five years ago, life for the residents of the small Yorkshire town Mopsworth had changed forever. It is now one of the best and happiest places in the world to live.

CHAPTER TWO

Murray looks at the photo on his desk of his best friends Benjy Twiglet, Elicia Twiglet, Rio and Sir Ralph being given their medals by the Queen of Mars after winning the Intergalactic Games. That day was one of the proudest moments in his life. Murray personally trained them with all the skills they needed to defeat the teams from all the other planets across the galaxy. After that he returned to Earth with them, or Puddle Planet as Earth is known on Mars to become the first Mars Ambassador to Earth.

Murray is looking at the Mars Embassy website to check the "How to find Mars Embassy on Earth" section was up to date. Queen Allison, the Queen of Mars is coming to visit Earth and he is sure the captain of the Royal Spaceship will ask for directions. Murray reads the words on the web page.

If you are approaching Puddle Planet with Jupiter on the left,

you need to aim for a small island called Great Britain. Great Britain is on the left of a country called France. (If you get it wrong and land in France by mistake you will know because when you open the main hatch their will be a very strong smell of garlic everywhere. If this happens close the main hatch and take off immediately) When you are flying over Great Britain you must look for a place called Mopsworth. Mopsworth is a small mining town in Yorkshire. Yorkshire is in the upper middle part of Great Britain (We are not sure exactly where). To help you, Mopsworth is about thirty miles from another place called Doncaster. If you are looking for Doncaster, it is about thirty miles away from Benjy and Elicia's house. Benjy and Elicia's house is in Mopsworth. From Benjy and Elicia's house you come out the front door, turn left, walk fifty-two steps up the road avoiding the lamp post, turn right at the red post box and the Mars Embassy is the green building in front of you."

P.S. - If you are arriving before lunch time, can you please pick me up a large Custardchinno and a Custard Danish Pastry...I will pay you back later.

Thanks a bunch

MURRAY   XXX

This all makes perfect sense to Murray.

To be honest, the location of the Mars Embassy was very controversial when it was built. Many of the world's leaders requested that the Mars Embassy be built in their capital city, including that silly man Ronald Dump from the United States. When he was the President of the United States he called and left so many messages on Murray's phone that Murray had all of Dump's calls redirected to the main sewage plant on the planet of Jupiter. The people of Jupiter are very big eaters. Therefore they are always on the toilet creating huge amounts of poo. So this means that the main sewage plant on Jupiter is always busy. No one ever has time to answer the phone at the sewage plant because they were either operating the poo pumps or on the loo themselves.

Murray had to admit it had been a great day when Dump was pushed out of office after he lost the US Presidential election. Murray had even done a little dance around his office in celebration. Dump was a very silly man. He claimed he had won, won, won and won by such a huge majority, but the rest of the world disagreed. He said his voters were the best voters in the world and that they would never let him loose. He had even said that as the US President he would make the Universe great again. But Murray thought that he only said this to try and make Murray feel warm and cuddly.

The good news is that since Dump lost his job as President of the US, he is now working as a golf caddy at one of his own golf courses just so that he can earn money to pay for the glue to keep the orange wig in place on top of his head. But Dump still has hope. He has applied for a job as a toilet cleaner at the White House. Why toilet cleaner? Well, when he read the government job vacancies list, he found that it was the only job he was qualified to do. So he has applied because he will do anything to get back inside the White House.

Unfortunately for Murray, Dump still likes to call and text Murray and see if he has found any more votes which he thinks he still needs to win the election. Dump insists that since it was a NASA Rocket that landed on Mars, it makes Mars the 51st State of America. Therefore all the votes on Mars should be given to him. If Murray could hurry up and send the votes, Dump said he will very happy and then he can still claim victory. Murray tries to point out that the election was last year and more importantly that people on Mars only vote on important issues such how many space slugs you are allowed to eat in one day, or how many asteroids you can legally own or even if it is OK to fart in a public spaceship. They have never voted on a leader for Earth. But this has not stopped Dump. He keeps on calling and texting Murray every day.

Today Murray is meeting Elicia Twiglet. Elicia is his official advisor on all Earth matters. Because she is one of his best friends, this is a great help. Today they are discussing setting up a super-market exchange program. The biggest supermarket operator on Mars is offering to open its first supermarket on Earth in Mops-worth and Earths biggest supermarket operator, Ballworts will open a supermarket in Greendung, the capital of Mars. This will be so that the people from both planets can try out each other's foods. Murray thinks that this is a super idea. Again many of the world's leaders have pointed out that Mopsworth is not the capital of Earth, and that the supermarket should be built in their capital city. Murray does not care. He wants his favourite Mars foods only a five minute's walk away.

CHAPTER THREE

Murray is sitting at desk when his secretary calls to inform him that Elicia is arriving for their meeting. Murray is still getting used to the idea of a having a secretary. It was Elicia's idea. On Mars no one has a secretary, all they do when they want something is to shout very loudly or ask a zombie to get it for them. On Mars every house or office has a zombie to do all the extra jobs. The zombies have been rescued from Pluto by the Martians. The reason for this is when the people of Pluto die, a couple of days later they wake up as zombies. They have nowhere to go. So Mars collects all the zombies up and gives them a job and a place to stay. They can even send their wages back to their families on Pluto who are still alive.

Even though the doors in the Mars Embassy are bigger than normal doors on Earth, Elicia stills has to stoop down to enter Murray's office. Elicia is the tallest person in Mopsworth. No one knows why she so tall or why she keeps growing. They say she is over seven and a half feet tall now, but no one is sure. She can change the lightbulbs in Mopsworth's lamp posts without a ladder and keeps her secret things on top of her wardrobe knowing her brother cannot find them, so she is very happy.

As Elicia walks in she is flanked by her own personal bodyguards, a group of battle-hardened chickens who are in the Chicken Special Forces. In Mopsworth, cows and chickens have equal rights to humans. As Mopsworth produces dairy free and egg free custard it seems the logical thing to do. Murray thinks that Elicia having bodyguards is very useful when he is talking with the world's leaders. They all seem so scared when they see a chicken holding a custard machine gun. He doesn't know why, but it has helped Murray and Elicia convince the world's leaders that Mopsworth is an excellent location for the world's first Mars Supermarket, and many other things that he wants to do.

'Good morning, Ambassador Murray' Elicia says as she sits down in a special chair made for her long legs. The Chicken Special Forces take their positions. Two chickens stand either side of her chair, one lies on the floor in a sniper position and the fourth hides behind a big rubber plant in stealth mode.

'It is a great morning Elicia. My queen is coming to visit me next week, and I am so excited. Her trip to earth is well timed. She will be arriving four weeks before Christmas. Earth will look beautiful with all the Christmas decorations and festive celebrations.'

'Yes, it is going to be a special time. I have the Queen Allison's itinerary. Would you like me to run through it with you?' asks Elicia.

'Yes, yes, yes, yesssssssssssssss,' says Murray with a huge smile. He starts to clap his hands and run around his desk. Once he has exhausted himself, Elicia begins to speak.

'The Queen Allison will arrive on Earth next Thursday. The journey from Mars will take seven minutes instead of the usual five minutes because the queen has requested to take the scenic route and circle the Earths moon and view Earth's flying antiques, which we call satellites.'

'I always wanted to ask. What do you have so many satellites?' asks Murray.

'Because every country wants to have a satellite in space. We use them for communications and looking at the other countries.'

'That is such a waste of time and creates so much rubbish. Once we decided to have only one leader on Mars, things became a lot easier. No more war or stopping each other from sending things from one place to the other. I can really recommend it.'

'Oh, I did not know that about Mars,' says Elicia writing all this information down

'And for your communications. If you built a 1,000km high arial at the North Pole and another at the South Pole the whole world could talk to each other and you would not need anything floating around in the sky. All those antiques are very dangerous when you are flying around having fun, I can tell you from experience. They need to all be put in big dustbin. Brought back down to Earth and squashed. You could the use the metal to make a million mugs for drinking hot chocolate. This would be much more useful.'

'Thank you, I will let the right people know,' says Elicia thinking that Murray sounds a bit mad today.

'Where will Queen Allison go first when she lands? Can you show everything on my new hologram blackboard?'

Elicia presses a button on her phone and the Queens trip itinerary appears in the air in the middle of the office. All the writing is in bright green because it is Murray's favourite colour.

'OK, Murray this is the plan so far, based on Queen Allison's wishes.'

Queen of Mars Earth Visit Itinerary - Wednesday 8th December

(Queen Allison's spaceship will take five minutes to fly from Mars to Earth due to its supersonic super-duper fast quantum drive rocket engines)

Day 1

07:50   Leave Mars
        - Queens Official Ear Wax Doctor to remove Royal Ear Wax
(helps for better hearing during the official visit to Puddle Planet)

07:55   Fly around Earth's Moon
        - Queen to take lots of Selfie Pics for her sister

07:56   View Flying Antiques (Earth's Satellites)
        - Take pictures to send to friends to make them laugh.

07:57   Fly to Mopsworth, UK.
        - Official Opening of the Mars Embassy
        - Meet Ambassador Murray and Lord Twiglet of Mopsworth
        - Leave holiday suitcases with Murray

09:00 Visit Snow White and the Seven Dwarves - State Visit
        - Meet with Snow White and the Seven Dwarves
        - Ask who is the fairest of them all to the Magic Mirror

10:00   Fly to White House, USA - State Visit
        - Meet the US President
        - Eat a hot dog with extra mustard

10:45   Fly to London, UK. State Visit to meet Queen of England
        - Game of Croquet with the Queen of England
        - Private Tour of the Tower of London by Sir Ralf, Queen's favourite Corgi dog.

11:45   Fly to Beijing, China, State Visit to meet President of China
        - Eat Presidential Chinese Dumplings
        - Fly up and down the Great Wall

12:30   Fly to Lapland, State Visit to meet Santa Claus
        - Ice skating with the Mrs. Claus
        - Go for a sleigh ride with Santa Claus

        - Visit Santa Claus's Grotto and give him a present wish list
        - Mince Pies and Hot Chocolate with Santa's Elves

14:30   Fly to Sherwood Forest
        - Land at Nottingham Castle
        - Meet Robin Hood and Maid Marian
        - Archery Lessons
        - Afternoon Tea in the Great Hall with the Sheriff of Nottingham

17:00   pm   Fly back to Mopsworth, UK.

17:30   pm   - Dinner with Ambassador Murray at the new Gragg Juice Cafe

19:00   pm   - Queen to take Royal Bubble Bath

19:30   pm   - Queen to receive Ear and Toe Massage

Day 2

09:00   - Key to the town of Mopsworth Presentation for Queen Allison
        - Drive around Mopsworth in a custard powered taxi
        - Visits Mopsworth Custard University and Custard Development Centre
13:00   Earth and Mars Technology Sharing Conference
        Location: Mopsworth Custard Theme Park
        Attending - All world leaders
        Mars Technology to give to Earth (Puddle Planet)
        - Flying Saucers Design powered by green snot
        - Intergalactic Spaceship Design
        - Teleportation Technology - for people only
        (travel from London to Sydney in 2 seconds)

        Earth Technology to give to Mars
        - Recipe for Custard Lickable Wall Paper
        - Pogo Sticks
        - Custard powered motorbikes
        - Electric Back scratchers
        - Leg Warmers
        - Umbrella Hats
        - Breathable Chocolate
        - Automatic Biscuit Tea Dunker
        - Radio Controlled Lawnmower
        - Microwave Popcorn

17:00   Fly to Bali - Start Holiday

Murray scratches his head. "Wow, that is a very busy schedule.'

'Yes, and after that, Queen Allison will go on holiday,' says Elicia. 'She tells me that she has not been on holiday for a long time.'

'True, it has been 322 years, I think. Queen Allison has not had a holiday since before the Great Saturn Wars. They were a long time ago, even before I was born. Where is the Queen going for her holiday?'

'Well,' said Elicia, ' I sent her all the holiday brochures I could find from our local travel agent. She has decided to go on holiday to Bali. This is her plan. I will put it on the screen.'

Queen of Mars Earth Visit Itinerary -
Friday 10th December - Sunday 8th January

09:00 **Go on Holiday** (First holiday for ages)
      - Fly Spaceship to Bali, Indonesia
      - Arrive a beach villa and unpack.
      - Holiday Activities
      Wind Surfing Lessons
      Balinese cookery classes with Benjy and Rio
      Balinese dance classes
      Yoga classes
      Kite flying lessons
      Swimsuit fashion show
      Sunbathing lessons
      Pie eating challenge
    Water skiing lessons
      Hand Gliding lessons
      Toenail cutting and nail painting class
      Visit to Balinese Volcano
      Visit to Balinese Temples (by car not spaceship)
      Visit to Sacred Balinese Waterfall
      Christmas Cake decorating lessons
      Christmas Tree decorating lessons
      Christmas Present wrapping lessons
      Christmas Cracker pulling lessons
      Christmas Pudding eating lessons
      Christmas Present opening lessons
      Christmas Present "Thank You" letter lessons

'Amazing', says Murray. 'What a holiday. I wish I was going. Maybe I can take a week's vacation and join her?'

'I don't think you will have time Ambassador Murray. The following week, after the Queens visit you must attend a meeting at

Hamley's Toy Shop in London. They are launching a new "Murray the Martian' toy for Christmas,' explains Elicia.

'Wow, what fun,' says Murray waving his arms around.

'After that you have to spend a day at the Mopsworth Custard Development Centre for Transport. They want to show you their latest inventions,' says Elicia.

'What have they invented this year?' says Murray, not sounding so happy at the thought of working for a whole day.

'Since the famous Professor Dan Garcia has joined the team, they have been very busy. The list is very extensive.'

New Custard Powered Transport

- Custard Passenger Jets
- Custard Powered Holiday Cruise Liners
- Custard Powered Formula 1 Racing Cars
- Custard Powered Snow plough - called the Custard Snow Buster
- Custard Powered Long Range Motorbikes
- Custard Powered Bicycles - for children only
- Custard Powered Milk floats
- Custard Powered Lawnmowers
- Custard Powered Delivery Trucks
- Custard Powered Tanks with Custard Cannon
- Custard Powered Police Vehicles with Custard Squirters

Murray scratches his head. 'The work of an Ambassador is never done.'

'Don't forget the other inventions that Professor Dan has been working on before he joined the transport section at the Mopsworth Custard Research Centre. They are revolutionary and are all the rage at the moment. Shops around the world cannot keep up with the demand, especially as we are only a few weeks away from Christmas. The Mopsworth Custard factory is working 24hrs a day to supply all the shops. They are the following,' says Elicia.

Mopsworth Custard New Products for Christmas:

- Custard Paper - Melt in Water to make a perfect drink. Perfect for travelers with a small suitcase.
- Custard Pens - to write on Birthday Cakes
- New Custard Flavours
    - Christmas Tree and Mince Pie Flavour
    - Gingerbread and Snowball Flavour - served cold
    - Christmas Pudding and Wrapping Paper Flavour
    - The Snowman - Chocolate Button, Carrot and Broom Flavour
    - Roast Turkey, Mash Potato and Brussels Sprout Flavour
    - Exploding Popcorn and Tartan Flavour - New Year's Eve Special
    - Bogey and Spaghetti Flavour - not a great seller
    - Stripy Rugby Sock Flavour
    - Football Boot and Grass Flavour
    - 100 Day Old Ear Wax Flavour - a Martian Favourite
    - Dinosaur Tail Flavour
    - Red Leicester Cheese, Pork Pie and Anchovy Flavour
    - Pea, Broccoli and Green Balloon Flavour (work in progress)
- Custard Lickable Wallpaper
    - Original Custard Flavour
    - Blueberry Flavour for boys
    - Raspberry Flavour for girls

Elicia continues. 'The Mopsworth Custard Research Centre is also working on a new Custard Computer Virus. The police requested a new weapon to use against international computer hackers. Things are progressing well. After the virus is uploaded to the computer the screen goes yellow. Professor Dan says is not finished yet. The police also want the virus to fill up the Hard Drive with custard as well and flood all the connected computers. Professor Dan says he is still working on it, but only at the weekends after eating a big bowl of custard for breakfast and playing football.'

'That is custardly fan daba dooooooozy,' says Murray with a big smile. 'Mopsworth Custard is changing the world. Okay, the last thing I want you to do is contact Captain Zac from Earths Space Rangers. Please ask him to confirm all security arrangements for the Queen's visit and holiday.'

'Of course,' says Elicia. 'I will contact Captain Zac immediately.'

Elicia stands up. Her bodyguards, the Chicken Special Forces fall in behind her as she leaves Murray's office

CHAPTER FOUR

It is only three days until the Queens Allison's visit. Mopsworth town is looking all sparkly with its Christmas lights. Outside the Mopsworth Custard Factory there is huge 100-foot Christmas tree. Placed on the tree is a present for every child in Mopsworth. It is a gift from the Mayor of Mopsworth to all the children.

Murray is feeling sad. His best friends in all the world, Benjy and Rio will not be with him when Queen Allison arrives in Mopsworth. Since returning to Earth from their trip to Mars, Benjy and Rio have moved to Bali in Indonesia. They have decided that they want to go to school where they can go to classes in the morning and surf in the afternoon. They have also opened a small beach cafe in Bali where they serve their favourite custard dishes to their school friends.

Murray thinks back to when he first met Benjy. They met when Benjy arrived at NASA's Mars Flight Program two years ago to work with Murray to make all the food for the first manned space mission to Mars. Benjy had won the Mopsworth Custard Space food competition, beating children from all over the world. The prize for first place was a place on the Mars Mission food production team.

Murray had already been working at NASA for a couple of years since his spaceship crashed on earth while he was on a quick trip to pick up a birthday present for his mum. After that he found out that NASA was planning a trip to Mars, so it was logical that he should join NASA so that they could help him to get home.

When Benjy joined NASA, he was accompanied by his sister Elicia, his best friend Rio and Sir Ralf, the Queen of England's favourite corgi dog. As a team they worked very hard to prepare all the different space foods for the astronauts. The only criteria that the food had to follow was that every meal had to include Mopsworth Custard.

Then one day, as they were loading the NASA spaceship with the astronauts food, Sir Ralph accidentally pressed a button and launched the spaceship. This sent all of them on a great journey to Mars.

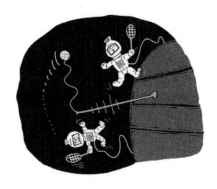

They all had a great time along the way playing games and trying to do scientific experiments. When the finally reached Mars, they all went to stay with Murray's parents. Luckily Murray's parents had a zombie helper, so lunch was soon served and Benjy, Elicia, Rio and Sir Ralf felt like part of the family.

The only problem the team from Earth had, in leaving Earth before time they only had half a tank of fuel. The fuel used in the NASA space rocket was a special blend of super charged Mopsworth Custard. The challenge for them was make more custard so they could return home. They eventually did this by entering and winning the Intergalactic Games. This was a shock to many of the other teams as they had never seen a team from Earth before.

Many said afterwards, it was beginners luck. The prize for winning was a huge dinosaur egg which the used to make gallons and gallons of fresh custard. Finally the team from Earth were able to fly home but not before they had flown around with rocket boots, seen flying saucers, met Queen Allison, the Queen of Mars and sampled Mar's most famous drink, a glass of Gragg juice.

But after all the hype and press attention when they returned to Earth, Benjy and Rio decided to move away from Mopsworth. So they are now living in Bali. There is also one extra benefit to living in Bali. They can now see one of the other contestants from the Mopsworth Custard Space Food Competition. His name is Iwan Salim, and he is from Indonesia. Benjy has always liked eating Iwan's Red Velvet Cake Custard Ball.

Well, at least the Queen Allison will have friends in Bali when she is on holiday. It is such a pity he is not joining her, Murray thinks. He would have been able to keep the Queen company and seen his best friends.

CHAPTER FIVE

In another part of the world, Dump is very happy. He has a new job. Today is his first day working back at the White House. The only downside is that he is only a junior White House toilet cleaner. But habits die hard, as soon as Dump starts work, he walks straight into the Oval Office, only to be pushed back out of the door. After being the US President for years, it is normal for Dump to walk straight into the Oval Office. Dump tries to explain to the big Secret Service agent guarding the office, that as the Ex-President this was a normal mistake. The secret service agent just growls at him.

Dump is told to only come back after the new US President has made a visit to the President's bathroom. This should not be long as the new US President is quite old, so he normally goes for a tinkle every twenty minutes. Some people say that the new US President is 110 years old. But Dump does not believe this and tells everyone that he must be lying about his age. The real reason that he says it is a lie is because he is no good at math and he cannot work out which year the new US President was born.

Dump is looking forward to going into the Presidential toilet. It was one of his favourite places to work when he was president. He had found that when he was sitting on the toilet, no one could look over his shoulder when he was writing a text or a tweet. This led to a few crazy messages being sent out during his time as president, especially if he rushed the message and pressed send before he flushed.

What Dump liked most about the bathroom were its facilities. It had a huge 120inch flat screen TV, a triple sink, a shower, a newspaper stand, a Cup Cake fridge, a coffee machine, an exercise bike and basketball hoop.

Dump had added even more facilities when he had become President to suit his personal needs. He had installed an industrial sized hair dryer, a tanning bed and a McDonald's kiosk filled with Big Macs, cheeseburgers and a McFlurry dispenser.

Dump decided that he had been the best president that the United States had ever had and, therefore after his additions, the Presidents toilet was the best toilet in the world.

CHAPTER SIX

The day has arrived for Queen Allison's visit to Earth. She wakes up in her Royal Palace on Mars, and squeals with excitement. All the Queen's advisors and all her zombie staff have been waiting for months for this day. Their days have been filled with preparations for the big trip. It has been all the Queen has talked about for months. She has been driving everyone completely bonkers. Two of her closest assistants have become so exhausted they have been sent for rest and cake eating therapy.

Her spaceship crew are also excited about their first trip to Earth. They have polished every inch of the spaceship inside and out by hand. It now shines so brightly under the Martian sun; it can be seen from the top of the Eiffel Tower in Paris.

◆ ◆ ◆

Waiting patiently in the grounds of the Mars Embassy in Mopsworth is Captain Zac. He is the man in charge of the Earth Space Rangers which is a newly formed military division at NASA. It was created after Benjy, Elicia, Rio and Sir Ralph's trip to Mars. Captain Zac is a hero. He is known for never feeling fear. He is the ultimate leader of his men who all love and respect him. He has been the British Army Chess Champion for the last four years. He can also drink a mug of custard in two seconds while standing on one leg while wearing flippers and playing the drums.

The Earth Space Rangers are made up from the best soldiers from all the countries in the world. The world's leaders felt that after official contact with Mars had been made, they needed to have a space force to defend earth and to also look good when they welcomed visitors from other planets. After Earth had won the Intergalactic Games, it was now the planet in the Universe that every alien wanted to visit. Earth expected many more visitors after Queen Allison's visit.

After the Earth Space Rangers had been formed, they spent 6 months training in the Atacama Desert in Chili, South America. Murray said that the Atacama Desert was the place that most reminded him of Mars, and Captain Zac did not disagree. After being in the Atacama Desert the Earth Space Rangers moved to Hollywood for close combat training. All the movie companies arranged for many of the most famous space movie films sets to be rebuilt with many of Hollywood's most famous actors playing the alien characters and taking on the roles of the enemy. For the last year Captain Zac and his rangers had battled against actors pretending to be Klingons, the Jem'Hadar, Darth Vader, E.T., Doctor Who, Batman, The Joker, Chewbacca, Rocket Raccoon, Spiderman, the Daleks, Yoda, the Blob, Jabba the Hutt, Zaphod Beeblebox, Predator, CP30 and R2D2, the Terminator, the BORG and the Tele Tubbies. It had been a challenging time, but now they felt they could face anything. Following their training the Earth Space Rangers have been put in charge of security for Queen Allison's visit. At this moment in time, Captain Zac has the most important job on Earth.

Captain Zac and his team wait silently by the green marble ornamental fountains for the first ever official state visit by a member of royalty from Mars. It is snowing, so everything is covered in a white blanket, including Earth's Space Rangers. All the Earth Space Rangers are cold, but not Captain Zac. He is wearing a short-sleeved space suit.

Standing on the front steps of the Mars Embassy is Ambassador Murray. He is waiting for waiting for his queen. He was also very excited and has the hugest grin. He was sure that his smile could be seen all the way from Venus. All the planning and phone calls with the world leaders, including a very long phone call with a dwarf called Dopey for over eight hours that had been very exhausting. Dopey was Snow Whites office assistant. Now all Murray needed to do was cross his fingers, toes and ears and hope that everything he and Elicia have planned will run like clockwork.

Behind Murray, Elicia stands with her clipboard in hand. She reads down the day's schedule one last time. Everything is in order. Even her security team have polished their beaks. Elicia is very proud of them.

Standing next to Elicia is her father, Lord Twiglet of Mopsworth. He is so proud of his daughter. She is the light of his life and even more important than his discovery of fresh custard.

Outside the garden walls of the embassy the people of Mopsworth wait with anticipation for the arrival of the royal spaceship.

CHAPTER SEVEN

Queen Allison is finishing her tour of the Earth antique satellites before landing on earth. She thinks the satellites all look very funny and the photographs she has taken will provide a very funny addition to her royal photo album. She instructs her spaceship captain to fly to Mopsworth as fast as he can.

The scene is beautiful as the Mars spaceship flies over Mopsworth. It is snowing. Christmas decorations are hanging on all the lampposts across town. Outside the town hall a 20ft Christmas tree dominates the market square. The queen pushes her camera against the spaceship window and takes lots of pictures.

In the gardens of the Mars Embassy in Mopsworth there is a big WHOOOOOOSH and all the snow is blown into the air as the Mars spaceship lands.

Captain Zac has never seen anything like it before in his life. The spaceship is bright green and shaped like a big beetle. It is the size of a twenty-storey building. There is a load bleeping noise, and a staircase silently unfolds below the spaceship. The Martian Royal Guard march out and surround the bottom of the stairs. The queen descends the stairs. She is wearing a green crown and carrying a green sceptre in her left hand.

Captain Zac and his Space Rangers salute Queen Allison as she puts her first foot on planet Earth.

'Welcome my Queen,' says Murray as he bows.

'Hello Murray, what a wonderful place you have here. It is so pretty,' Queen Allison replies, waving her sceptre.

Murray stands back from the main entrance. Across the doorway is thick green ribbon.

'Dear Queen, will you please do me the honour of cutting the ribbon and officially opening the first Mars Embassy on earth.'

'Of course Murray. Give me the scissors.'

Murray hands Queen Allison a pair of green scissors. She cuts the ribbon, and a huge cheer rings our from all the Embassy staff and the people of Mopsworth outside the embassy's garden walls.

'Now that is done, let us all have a cup of this famous Yorkshire tea that I have been hearing so much about,' Queen Allison says.

Queen Allison links arms with Lord Twiglet as she charges

inside the embassy. 'I want to hear all the news about Benjy and Rio,' says Queen Allison.

◆ ◆ ◆

After spending time with Murray, Elicia and Lord Twiglet discussing her trip, Queen Allison decides it is time to leave. She is looking forward to meeting Snow White and the Seven Dwarfs. Her advisors have told her they are the most famous people on Earth. The Queen Of Mars has read all their books and watched all their films in preparation for the meeting. She thinks Snow White is very beautiful and the dwarves are all very funny. She just hopes that she does not meet the Evil Queen. She seems a bit scary.

Queen Allison has also insisted that her holiday suitcases are left behind at the embassy during her visit to the world leaders as they take too much room in her spaceship. As soon as Murray agrees, piles of suitcases are dumped on the ground in front of the embassy. Immediately the embassy staff start to carry them inside. There are so many cases they fill all the storage cupboards, the dining room, the ball room, the guest bedrooms, the guest bathrooms, the swimming pool, the bowling alley, the garden shed, the dog kennel, the fridge, and the freezer. How many things does a queen need to take on holiday, Murray thinks?

Before Queen Allison leaves to go to the next destination, Captain Zac suggests they go on his Earth Space Ranger spaceship for security reasons and even makes a funny Grrrrrhing noise when the engines are started that many people think is very cute. It has been programmed with all the queens trip destinations. But he admits his spaceship is a lot smaller than the Queens.

The Queen thinks about this, and although it is a very kind offer, she likes her own spaceship more. She explains her ship is quicker and more comfortable, plus better food and better video games like "Attack Earth". She apologies for the title of the video game as it was made before Mars became friends with earth, but it is a brilliant game with 3,844 levels.

So after a few minutes of discussion with the Directors of NASA, Captain Zac and his Rangers join the Queen of Mars on her spaceship. As soon as the door is closed the spaceship rises up into the air.

CHAPTER EIGHT

The weather in the Black Forest of Germany is the same as in Mopsworth. The Black Forest is covered in a blanket of snow, but here the sun is out and there is not a cloud in the sky. The spaceship quickly lands, and stairs are lowered to the ground.

A red carpet is quickly rolled out by the seven dwarfs. It takes longer than expected a Dopey tries to roll the carpet the wrong way.

Waiting to greet Queen Allison, is Snow White and her handsome Prince standing on a red podium. Beside the podium the seven dwarfs line up after their carpet laying duty. Captain Zac and ten of his best space rangers form a guard of honour for Queen Allison. The rest of Captain Zac's rangers take strategic positions around the Black Forest.

Snow White, the handsome Prince and the seven dwarfs are wearing their best Christmas outfits. They all wave hello as Queen Allison approaches.

The official visit to the seven dwarfs cottage goes fantastically well. They show Queen Allison where they all sleep and which place, they sit at for meals. Queen Allison also loves visiting the dwarfs diamond mine. She goes down inside the mine and up again to the surface on their little train five times.

After the visit to the mine, they all walk to the castle. This is the part Queen Allison has been looking forward to. Inside a special room is the Magic Mirror. Queen Allison stands in front of the mirror and asks the question.

'Mirror, Mirror on the wall, who is the greenest person of all?' asks Queen Allison.

'My Queen, you are the fairest and greenest here, it is true. But Snow White is a thousand times more lovely, fair and beautiful than you'.

Queen Allison starts laughing as she turns to face Snow White. 'This mirror knows who is boss.'

Before leaving the queen has a snowball fight against the seven dwarfs. All is going well until Dopey starts throwing snowballs at the other dwarves and the snowball fights descends into chaos.

Snow White and the handsome Prince are perfect hosts. The Queen is so happy that she invites Snow White, the handsome Prince and all the dwarfs including Dopey to come and stay at her Royal Palace in Greendung, the capital of Mars after she has returned home.

Elicia oversees presents for Queen Allison's trip. She has prepared gifts for all the state visits.

Queen Allison gives Snow White a large necklace maid of Martian gold and in return receives a sack of diamonds from the dwarfs mine.

Queen Allison's spaceship takes off and shoots straights up into the sky. Next on the royal tour is a visit to the President of the United States. Captain Zac is just fastening his seatbelt when the spaceship starts to descend.

Spaceship tannoy. "WE ARE NOW APPROACHING THE WHITE HOUSE. PREPARE FOR LANDING".

Captain Zac is shocked. It has only been two minutes and they have already travelled 4,088 miles. He cannot believe how fast the Mars spaceship is.

The President of the United States is waiting on the front lawn of the White House with all his office staff. His favourite Presidential helicopter is on the lawn in front of him. They have allocated a parking space to the left of the helicopter for the Earth Space rangers spaceship to land. The plan is to have a photograph of the Earth spaceship and the President's helicopter with the US President and Queen Allison side by side after the spaceship lands.

In the sky above Washington, the Mars spaceship approaches. Everyone is shocked at its size. Where is the small Earth spaceship that was planned to carry the Queen of Mars? Oh no, everyone on the lawn realises there is not enough space for the Mars spaceship and the President's helicopter. As the Mars spaceship lands it squashes the President's helicopter like a pancake. The US President starts crying.

The door of the Mars spaceship opens, and the silent ladder unfolds itself. The Queen of Mars descends from her spaceship with a huge smile on her face, filled by Elicia. Captain Zac and his team form a guard of honour. She sees the US President crying. She has no idea what is wrong but gives him a big hug anyway.

'It is so nice that you are so happy to see me. I was very worried before the trip that you didn't like Martians. Can I ask is that why you are crying?' the Queen of Mars enquires.

The US President nods. He is too embarrassed to tell her the truth.

Queen Allison spins around to tell Elicia that she thinks the US President is very sweet. As Queen Allison does this, her bottom is so big that it swats the US President out of the way like a fly. He lands face down on the White House lawn.

'What are you doing down there?' the Queen asks looking at the US President in surprise.

'Nothing,' replies the President. 'I was just checking the length of the White House grass.' He is too scared to tell Queen Allison her bottom is too big.

◆ ◆ ◆

A few minutes later Queen Allison and the US President are sitting in the Oval office eating hotdogs and drinking a big glass of cola. The President is explaining that hotdogs are his country's national meal. They discuss spaceship design and Queen Allison promises to provide NASA with all the technical plans for long range spaceships, flying saucers for local travel and their revolutionary teleport system.

Then it is time to go. The next stop on Queen Allison's tour is to visit another queen, the Queen of England.

Before Queen Allison leaves, she asks to go to the toilet in the Presidents bathroom. The US President says yes and tells her she must take as long as she needs. He then worries what she will do in his private bathroom. How do Martians go to the toilet? Will she make a big mess and leave a funny smell? Never mind he thinks, whatever happens he has his new toilet cleaner to clean up whatever mess Queen Allison leaves behind. He has Ex-President Dump to do all the cleaning up. He laughs as he thinks this is very funny.

The Queen Allison is in the toilet for a full fifteen minutes. When she comes out, she explains that the reason she took so long is that she sent a video of her time in the bathroom to her sister back on Mars. She also shot a couple of hoops with the basketball and ate a cheeseburger.

Before she leaves, Queen Allison gives the US President a large piece of Martian rock for his mantel piece. He in return gives her a baseball bat, ball, and mitt.

Queen Allison is soon back on her spaceship and over halfway to London before she realises that she has her video communicator behind in the US President's bathroom.

Oh well Queen Allison thinks, she has another communicator in her handbag. A Martian queen always needs to have back up.

Back inside the White House, Dump is mopping the floor and washing the walls of the US Presidents bathroom. There is green slime and pieces of hotdog everywhere.

Dump closes the bathroom door. He does not want anyone to see him on his hand and knees scooping up the green slime with his hands and putting it into a bucket.

CHAPTER NINE

The Mars spaceship lands on the lawn of Buckingham Palace in London. A soon as it touches down the Queen of England's corgis dogs run up to the spaceship to welcome Queen Allison.

The Queen of England has arranged for both queens to play a game of croquet which is traditionally an Irish game, but the Queen of England says they stole it hundreds of years ago from the Irish and refuse to give it back.

After croquet, Queen Allison is taken on a private tour of the Tower of London by Sir Ralph, the Queen of England's favourite. Sir Ralph has met Queen Allison before when he visited Mars with Benjy, Elicia and Rio. Queen Allison gives Sir Ralph a special blue tablet that enables him to speak and explain the history of the Crown Jewels in the Tower of London and all about the people that had their heads lopped off after spending time in the tower's prison.

Before Queen Allison leaves, she announces that London will be twinned with Greendung, the capital of Mars. There are huge cheers from all the staff at Buckingham Palace and the two queens dance a waltz to celebrate their union.

The two queens exchange presents. Queen Allison gives the Queen of England a huge green Martian emerald stone, the size of a rugby ball and suggests it could be used for a new crown. The Queen of England gives Queen Allison a Christmas Food Hamper from Harrods with all Britain's most famous foods, plus a new diamond tiara she had specially made for Queen Allison's head.

CHAPTER TEN

The next destination on Queen Allison's world tour is Beijing in China. The Mars spaceship lands in the center of Tiananmen Square, next to the entrance to the Forbidden City.

There are three thousand Red Army soldiers waiting to greet Queen Allison. After they parade up and down for half an hour the President of China stops the marching because Queen Allison has fallen asleep.

The President of China then invites Queen Allison to walk through the Forbidden City and sample his favourite mushroom dumplings.

The visit to China is finished off with a fly over of the Great Wall of China. Queen Allison thinks that the Great Wall is magnificent and takes hundreds of pictures. Maybe she will build a similar wall outside Greendung.

Before Queen Allison leaves, she exchanges gifts. President of China offers a box of a 1,000 Moon cakes before bowing. Queen Allison in return gives him a pair of slippers made out of Martian gold.

The Mars spaceship fly's off to its next destination.

CHAPTER ELEVEN

The skies are clear as the Mars spaceship swoops down towards Lapland. To Queen Allison's great excitement, her spaceship is escorted into land by Santa Claus on his flying sleigh pulled by his wonderful reindeer.

Both the Queen Allison's spaceship and Santa Claus's sleigh land side by side. The reindeer are a bit scared of the big spaceship, but Santa Claus calms them down by giving them all a mince pie each to eat.

The first thing Queen Allison does is to go ice skating with Mrs. Claus while Santa Claus goes to check on his elves. Christmas is only a few weeks away and he needs to make sure all the presents are being made correctly and following all the "Christmas Wish Lists" he has been given to him by children from all over the world.

Ice skating is not easy, but Mrs. Claus is a good teacher and soon Queen Allison is zooming across the ice lake, screaming with delight.

Next Queen Allison is taken on a sleigh ride by Santa Claus. They fly once around the world. Queen Allison realises that Santa's sleigh is just as fast as her spaceship but it is open top, so a lot colder.

Returning back to Lapland, Queen Allison is invited to Santa's workshop and she sits by a big fire drinking hot chocolate while all the elves show her all the presents they have been making for the children.

Finally, Queen Allison visits Santa Claus in his Grotto. He invites Queen Allison to sit on his lap and tell him what she wants for Christmas. This is not easy as she is a lot bigger than the children that normally sit on his knee. Queen Allison thinks very hard about what she wants for Christmas, and then tells Santa she would like a packet of Saturn Bubble Gum. She says that whoever eats the bubble gum can breath out fire like a dragon. This present will be a challenge Santa thinks and will require a trip to another planet. But a wish is a wish, and he will try his best to find a packet and make Queen Allison happy on Christmas day.

It is time for the gift exchange. Queen Allison gives Santa Claus and Mrs. Claus a flying saucer. She says that it will give the reindeer a rest. Santa Claus gives Queen Allison a sack full of toys for any children she may meet before Christmas.

After waving goodbye to Santa Claus, Mrs. Claus and the elves Queen Allison pulls out a cloak, puts on a small pair of glasses, draws a jagged scar on her forehead and tells her captain to fly her towards Sherwood Forest.

CHAPTER TWELVE

As the spaceship approaches Nottingham Castle, which is next to Sherwood Forest, Queen Allison gets very excited. She starts shouting **SHAZAM,** and **LEGS OF A SPIDER**. The crew of the spaceship are all very confused but say nothing.

The spaceship lands inside the castle walls. Waiting to meet

Queen Allison is the Sheriff of Nottingham in all his finery.

'Welcome Queen,' says the Sheriff of Nottingham.

'Where is Robin Hood and Maid Marian?' Queen Allison asks looking over his shoulder.

'Oh, they live in Sherwood Forest, outside the castle walls. You see, we are not really the best of friends,' the Sheriff explains.

'OK, I see. Well I must be off. I will be back for later for dinner. And don't forget to have that young wizard boy sitting next to me' Queen Allison says as she marches off out the main gate of the castle.

The Sheriff is left standing with his open mouth in shock. He is also thinking who the young wizard boy could be?

Queen Allison turns to Captain Zac who is running to catch up. 'Captain Zac, please lead the way,'

'Yes, your Highness. I. believe he lives under a tree called the Great Oak,' replies Captain Zac.

Elicia looks at Captain Zac and gives him the thumbs up to confirm the location.

Twenty minutes later Queen Allison, Elicia and Captain Zac are standing under the branches of the Great Oak. Robin Hood, Maid Marian and all Robin's Merry Men are fast asleep after eating a heavy lunch and snoring very heavily. The noise is painful to Queen Allison's ears.

'Wake Up!!!' says Captain Zac in a very loud voice. 'Queen Allison wishes to speak with you.'

Robin Hood wakes up and rubs his eyes. Standing front of him is a seven-foot-tall green woman wearing a black cape and small glasses. Next to her is equally tall young woman with a clipboard.

'Who wants to speak with me?' asks Robin Hood.

'The Queen of Mars', replies Captain Zac. 'You were meant to be waiting at Nottingham Castle today for her arrival. My notes tell me that Elicia confirmed everything with you last week.'

'Oh, I thought that was a joke. She said a Martian was coming to visit me from another planet,' says Robin Hood, roiling over to go back to sleep.

The Queen of Mars is getting angry. 'I am not a joke. I am standing here in front of you and yes, I am a Martian. I am also a queen and can have you thrown into prison and made to cut the toenails of zombies for eternity if I want to. But right now I would like you to teach me how to use a bow and arrow. I would also like Maid Marian to teach me how to my braid hair. Is that too much to ask?'

Robin Hood is shocked and apologises. 'I am so sorry your Highness. Little John, fetch me my bow and my best arrows. I have to teach a queen how to become as good an archer as my Merry Men.'

After Queen Allison has fired over a hundred arrows, she is now starting to hit her target. A few of her early shots have sent Robin Hood's Merry men running for cover. Following this, the queen spent a long time have her hair brushed and braided by Maid Marian. It was not easy for Maid Marian to do this and it made her very tired. Martian hair is like wire and Maid Marian has to use a big stick to help twist and bend the hair.

Once Queen Allison has left Robin Hood and Maid Marian, they shake their heads. What a strange afternoon they have had. It was the first time they had ever met a seven-foot-tall green Martian woman. They hope it is the last time as well as neither of them ever want to be made to cut a zombies toenail, whatever a zombie was.

Queen Allison's feelings towards Robin Hood and Maid Marian were the same. No time was too soon, but she did like his green outfit.

On retuning back to Nottingham Castle, Queen Allison goes straight into the Great Hall and sits down. The Sheriff of Nottingham instructs his staff to bring out the food.

'So where is the boy wizard?' asks Queen Allison.

'We don't have a boy wizard. If you want magic, I can call Merlin. But he lives in Camelot, so it would take a couple of days for him to ride here on his horse,' says the Sheriff.

'Merlin, I don't want Merlin,' says Queen Allison in an exasperated voice. 'I want to meet that young boy with the wand who fights dragons and trolls.'

The Sheriff of Nottingham smiles. At last, he can get one over this rude green queen.

'Sorry, you have the wrong castle and the wrong story. Anyway, he lives in a school, not a castle. I know his school looks like a castle. But it really isn't. His school is much nicer than this cold and old building. But this is home and I love it,' says the Sheriff.

Queen Allison is very angry. She really wanted to meet the boy wizard. She has been practicing with a chopstick for weeks, waving it around her head and pointing it at her staff.

Now she wants to shoot the Sheriff with her ray gun. But she knows Captain Zac and Elicia will get upset, and it is not a very friendly thing to do.

'Oh well Sheriff, I must be off,' Queen Allison says as she picks up a whole leg of lamb and eats it in one mouthful. After a lot of chewing she spits out a completely clean bone. It is shiny and white with not a single piece of meat left on it.

'Ta, Ta.' says Queen Allison as she runs back to her spaceship with, Elicia, Captain Zac and his space rangers close behind. No gift for him thinks Queen Allison.

CHAPTER THIRTEEN

Queen Allison finally lands back in Mopsworth. It has been a very long day and the busiest day she has had in the last hundred years. She is exhausted and very tired.

Before Queen Allison can rest, Murray takes her on a tour of the Mopsworth Custard Factory and the Mopsworth Custard Theme Park. Queen Allison is too tired to go on any rides even though the rollercoaster looks to be a lot of fun.

Before going back to the Mars Embassy Queen Allison and Murray stop at the newly opened Guzgloop Cafe. Queen Allison orders a large glass of Gragg Juice. It is a nice way to end the day she thinks.

While they are resting in the cafe, Murray asks why Queen Allison has turned down the invitation to visit the President of Russia. Queen Allison replies by saying that he had invited her to go brown bear hunting in Siberia. This was the coldest part of Russia. Queen Allison thought about it but decided that she likes brown bears and also warm toes, so the answer had been no.

Back at the Mars Embassy Queen Allison thinks her first day on Earth has been a great success. She has ridden a mining train, squashed a helicopter, fired arrows, eaten a hot dog, and shot hoops. It was a pity that she did not meet the boy wizard, but maybe Elicia can sort that out.

Queen Allison then takes a long "Pea and Spinach" bubble bath before climbing into bed. She is exhausted. After that she has her ear and toe massage and falls asleep with a smile on her face.

CHAPTER FOURTEEN

The following day Queen Allison eats her first Full English Breakfast. After breakfast Queen Allison is taken to the center of Mopsworth where she is handed the Key to the Town of Mopsworth by the Mayor. After receiving the key she is driven around Mopsworth in an open top taxi powered by custard. All the residents of Mopsworth town have come out and wave yellow and green flags as she passes by.

Then it is off to meet Professor Dan at the Mopsworth Custard University and Custard Development Centre. For this part of her tour, Queen Allison will be accompanied by Elicia and Lord Twiglet who is the Managing Director of the Mopsworth Custard Company. It has been said that without her father's discovery, the world may have been denied dairy free fresh custard.

They arrive at the Mopsworth Custard University and Custard Development Centre. Elicia's Chicken Special Forces have cleared a path from the Mopsworth Custard taxi to the entrance of the Custard Development Centre.

Professor Dan is in his laboratory conducting an experiment when Queen Allison arrives. The laboratory is filled wall to wall with different experiments. There are glass jars and demijohns bubbling away with a multitude of different colours. Bunsen burners keeping the heat constant under each experiment. In the corner, there is a large tank of Mopsworth Custard that is feeding all the experiments with fresh custard.

Captain Zac is worried for Queen Allison's safety in case there is an explosion. Everything seems to be rattling and shaking as steam and gasses escape into the air.

Professor Zac appears from behind a particularly large glass jar.

'Aha, welcome to my laboratory,' Professor Dan says as he bows to Queen Allison.

Professor Dan is a lot younger than Captain Zac has anticipated. In fact, Professor Dan is a child prodigy. He is only twelve years old. But already, Professor Dan is already the leading custard product inventor in the world, and maybe the universe. One of the main reasons for this is that he loves custard. Making new custard flavours and inventing new uses for custard is something that comes very easily to Professor Dan. At night he goes to sleep dreaming of new things he can make from custard. Sometimes his mother finds him sleepwalking in the middle of the night saying the word custard over and over again.

'Can you guess what I am working on today?' Professor Dan says pointing towards his experiment.

Queen Allison and her group all lean in and stare at the experiment. All they can see are bedsheets and pillowcases boiling away in big pot filled with a yellow and red stripy liquid. The group admit, they have no idea.

'It's a new concept I am trying out,' says Professor Dan as he stirs the bed sheets, pillowcases and the yellow and red mixture together with a big wooden spoon.

'What is it?' enquires Elicia. She is very curious to know. If it is something good, she will try and buy it for her brother Benjy for Christmas.

'Custard beds sheets,' says Professor Dan very proudly. 'If I can get the formula right, children can sleep with the aroma of custard all around them.'

'That sounds amazing,' says Elicia.

'It needs more work. I have the aroma spot on, but I have one small problem. I tested the sheets last week on my sister. When she woke up she was completely yellow. It took my dad all day to wash it off.'

'So work in progress,' says Queen Allison.

'Yes, but I have lots of other things to show you,' says Professor Dan.

For the next hour, Professor Dan amazes his guests with all his new inventions. Queen Allison particularly likes the Bogey and Spaghetti Flavoured custard and asks for a jar to take home.

Following lunch, Queen Allison is the Keynote Speaker at Mars and Earth Technology Sharing Conference. After her speech, Queen Allison leaves her best Mar's scientists to discuss sharing and exchanging technology with all the Earth's best scientists. It is a very successful conference. The only thing Queen Allison is not sure about is what Martians will do with the leg warmers. Maybe they will give them to their zombie servants as their annual bonus.

Queen Allison hopes that the next time she is back on Earth that she will see flying saucers everywhere instead of cars. They are a lot more environmentally friendly and can be fuelled by any rotting fruit or even old shoes. Queen Allison has even seen one powered by old traffic cones and wet underpants, but it did not fly very fast. Perhaps Queen Allison thinks, her flying saucers can be adapted to be powered by custard?

It is now holiday time. Queen Allison is so excited. She is standing next to her spaceship waiting to board. She is already dressed in her swimsuit, wearing orange flippers and using her new sunglasses. This looks a little odd to everyone as it still snowing in Mopsworth.

Queen Allison can wait no longer. She blows Murray and Elicia a few kisses and runs up the stairs into her spaceship.

Murray, Elicia and all the staff of the Mars Embassy wave goodbye as the Mars spaceship rises up into the sky and races off towards Bali.

'Now we can all relax,' says Murray with a big grin on his face. 'The next thing we have to look forward too is Christmas in two weeks. All I am going to do between now and Christmas Eve is sit in front of the fire and eat mince pies covered in Dinosaur Tail flavoured custard.'

'Don't forget your trip to Hamleys toy shop and your day with Professor Dan,' Elicia reminds him.

'OK, but I am not going to Hamleys until I have eaten at least a thousand mine pies,' says Murray.

Elicia thinks that Murray is mad with his food combinations. But he is correct about one thing. It is time for her to put her feet up as well. She is exhausted after Queen Allison's trip. She hopes that Captain Zac and his rangers will not become too tired looking after Queen Allison as she participates in all her holiday activities.

CHAPTER FIFTEEN

Back on Mars, all the government staff are celebrating that Queen Allison is on holiday. This means they are also on holiday. HOORAY, they all cheer.

As a present to her staff for all their hard work, Queen Allison has given all her Royal Palace staff, Members of Mars Parliament, Regional Governors, City Mayors, Town Mayors, Village Mayors, all public workers, Head Boys, Head Girls, School Prefects, Football Team Captains, Playing Card box packers, Gragg Jockeys, Wet Sock Squeezers and Dragons a three-day holiday.

There is now a huge party in Greendung's largest venue, the "Great Martian Hall". The hall is so big it can fit a million Martians inside doing headstands. Inside, tables are piled high with the best

Martian cakes and biscuits. To wash it all down there are 300 barrels of Martian Giggle Juice, a favourite at Martian parties.

As everyone is dancing and laughing from drinking too much giggle juice, the lights in the Great Martian Hall suddenly go out. Then the music goes silent.

The doors at the end of the hall opens. In the entrance stands a female zombie. Behind her stand a hundred more zombies armed with ray guns.

In a very slow voice the female zombie speaks.

'MY...NAME...IS...STEP-H..I..AM....THE...LEADER...OF...THE... ZOMBIE...ACTION...PARLIAMENT...WE....ARE....CALLED....ZAP'

'What do you want?' shouts a Martian from the crowd.

Step-H continues her speech.
'YOU...ARE...NOW....OUR...PRISONERS......YOU..WILL...
STAY....LOCKED...IN....THIS....HALL...WE...WILL...NOT...BE...
YOUR...SLAVES...ANY...MORE.....WE...HAVE...TAKEN....OVER...
MARS.'

The doors then close leaving all the Martian government and all government employees trapped inside the hall.

Three hours later after a very slow walk (fast for a zombie), Step-H sits on the throne inside the Royal Palace of Mars. She is chewing on an old shoe. The shoe tastes wonderful, especially the laces. The reason of this is that zombies on Mars do not like eating people or drinking their blood. But they do love eating other people's shoes. The oldest, and smelliest shoes are the best.

She picks up the phone and calls the Royal Spaceship. The call is picked up straight away by the spaceship captain.

'Royal spaceship. Captain speaking. How can I help?' the captain says into his space communicator.

'QUEEN......I.....WANT....SPEAK....TO....QUEEN,' Step-H says as fast as she can.

'I am sorry she is very busy right now. She has just entered a swimsuit competition and she is doing very well. I do not want to disturb her,' the captain replies.

'I...AM...THE...NEW...LEADER....OF....MARS...WE...ARE...ZAP...

THE ZOMBIES....ARE....IN.....CONTOL,' Step-H says as fast as she can.

'Zombies, in control? I think you are a bit mad. Zombies are not in control of Mars. Queen Allison is the leader of Mars,' the captain says.

'NOT....NOW....I....AM...THE...NEW....LEADER...THE..... QUEEN...MUST....RETURN...AND...BECOME.....MY...PRISONER... NOW.', Step-H demands.

'Prove that this is not a crank call,' demands the captain.

Step-H slowly presses a button on her phone and sends a picture of all the Martians locked up inside the Great Martian Hall.

The captain receives the picture. 'Oh dear,' he says.

'TELL......QUEEN....COME....BACK....NOW,' says Step-H. The call is ended.

The captain stares at the phone for a few minutes. He then runs out of the spaceship and along the beach to find the swimsuit contest.

The Queen of Mars is sitting in the captain's chair on her spaceship. She calls Step-H on a video call.

'HELLO......WHO.....IS......THIS?' Step-H says, looking very gormless.

'This is your queen. Release my staff immediately,' demands Queen Allison.

'NO….NO…NO,' says Steph-H. 'YOU…COME….HOME….NOW.'

'Not on your nelly. I am the Queen of Mars and I am having too much fun on my holiday.'

'I…AM….IN….CHARGE…OF….MARS…NOW….I…AM…YOUR… LEADER,' says Step-H.

'Don't be silly. You are a zombie. Release my staff. I will deal with you when I come home after my holiday. I sentence you to a thousand years washing up in my kitchens when I catch you,' says Queen Allison.

'NO….IF…YOU…DO…NOT…COME…HOME…I   WILL…FORCE… YOUR….STAFF…TO…DRINK…GIGGLE….JUICE…UNTIL….THEY….GO…MAD…WITH…LAUGHTER…'

Step-H ends the call.

◆ ◆ ◆

The Queen of Mars is angry that her holiday is being ruined by this crazy zombie. She instructs the spaceship captain to call all the offices telephone numbers in the Mars Palace and Parliament building to see if the zombies are really in control.

The queen thinks that the call from Step-H is really a big joke created by her staff to have some fun. She thinks that it is impossible for zombies to have taken over Mars.

The queen leaves the spaceship and goes back to her swimsuit competition. She is hoping to win.

CHAPTER SIXTEEN

Just like the Queen of Mars, Dump is having a terrible day as well. He is locked inside the Presidents bathroom. He has been banging on the door for hours and shouting for help. No one replies. What can he do? If he is stuck in the bathroom for the Christmas holidays, will wonders if he will survive?

He looks around the bathroom. He thinks he will be OK. There are enough cheeseburgers, muffins, and pots of ice cream for him to eat. He has a huge TV, a shower, and a toilet.

But Dump is still very upset. He hates it when he talks, and no one hears him or tells him how great he is. He has been talking to the bathroom mirror for over half an hour and all the man in the mirror does is copy him. The mirror man says nothing new. It is infuriating. So he decides he will not talk to the mirror man anymore.

As Dump continues to clean the bathroom he suddenly cheers. He has found a mobile phone. He has no idea who it belongs to. He hopes he can call someone on the outside and tell them to release him.

Then Dump has a better idea. He will record a video message and send it to all the contacts on the phone. First, he needs a hat. He remembers one of his old campaign hats is hanging in the centre of the toilet's dartboard. It is one of his favourites with a slogan that says, "In America - We Love a Good Dump".

Dump finds the video button and presses record. 'Hello, this is Dump....your best, your most favourite President ...Sorry I mean your Ex-President, but not for long...Hehehe....Anyway, I need your help....I am locked inside the Presidents private toilet in the White House....I have been banging on the door...but no one answers me....I don't think they like me very much...I have even spoken to the man in the mirror....he is no help at all...Please can you call the Secret Service and tell them I am here....In fact don't tell them it's me. They don't like me either....Just tell anyone you know that there is a man stuck in a toilet....Then with your help I can be free...We can then make me, and America Great Again....Thank you and please hurry as my hair is going very floppy.'

Dump is very happy with his message. He thinks he looks super cool in the video. He goes to the address book and sees there are only six numbers. They are "Sister", "Sister 2", "Happy Mother", "Angry Mother", "Ear Lobe Massager", and "Office Slave".

Dump cannot choose, so he sends the video message to all six numbers

Unbeknown to Dump the MESSAGE IS SENT TO MARS...NOT EARTH

On Mars, Step-H receives a message on her phone telling her she has a new video message. She opens the message and plays the video.

'ERRR...THIS...IS...GREAT,' Steph-H says out loud. 'HE.... SOUNDS...JUST...LIKE...ME,'

Steph- H shows the video to her other members of ZAP. Zombies like Dump as he sounds so stupid.

Step-H calls Dump. Dump is very excited and answers the call straight away.

'Hi, this is Ex-President Dump. Who are you?' Dump says into the phone.

'WE...ARE....ZAP....We...WILL...HELP...YOU...WE...HAVE... TAKEN...OVER...MARS...IF....YOU...CAN...HELP...US...CAP- TURE...THE...QUEEN...OF...MARS...WE...WILL...RE- LEASE....YOU.'

Dump looks at the phone confused. He has never heard of ZAP. Is it a new division of the US Secret Service?

'Who is ZAP?' Trump asks.

'ZOMBIE...ACTION...PARLIAMENT.....WE...ARE...THE...NEW... LEADERS...OF...MARS,' says Step-H.

'Oh, so you are powerful people then,' says Dump. He decides to negotiate. 'OK, ZAP. If I help you to capture the Queen of Mars, I want something in return.'

'WHAT...DO...YOU...WANT?' says Step-H.

Dump tells Step-H that if he helps ZAP to capture the Queen of Mars, he wants ZAP to help him become the US President again.

'OK...WE...WILL...DO...THAT.' Step-H says.

'Fantastic...between the zombies on Mars and myself, we will make America Great Again!' Dump says as he starts doing a silly dance around the Presidents toilet.

◆ ◆ ◆

Outside the Presidential bathroom everything is quiet. The Oval office is empty. After the visit from the Queen of Mars, the US President left to go on holiday for Christmas. He is planning to be on holiday for over four weeks. This will also give him time to get over the loss of his squashed helicopter.

All the US Presidents staff have left for their holidays as well. Therefore no one misses Dump or realises that he is locked in the Presidents bathroom.

CHAPTER SEVENTEEN

Queen Allison is happily enjoying her holiday. She has not replied to the request by ZAP and Step-H. In fact she is having so much fun, she has forgotten all about the zombies taking over Mars.

Even when her captain mentions it, she thinks that it is still just a big joke being played on her by her staff back on Mars.

On Mars, Step-H is getting angry. 'NOT....HAPPY....NOT....HAPPY.....NOT......HAPPY.'

Step-H keeps looking at her mobile phone. 'BAD.....
QUEEN......BAD.....QUEEN.' Steph-H sits down at the Queen's desk
and types out a message to the Queen's spaceship. She gives the
queen one last ultimatum.

**Queeeeen, where are you? Tell ZAP where we can
find you? You must return back to Mars now. If
you do not reply, we will forcibly bring you back
to Mars. You have ten minutes to reply.**

From,

ZAP, the new rulers of Mars.

Step - H sends the email and waits. She waits and waits and
waits. To distract herself, Step-H starts chewing an old shoe. It is
her third shoe of the day. Being the leader of a planet is very stress-
ful and shoe chewing was a great help.

There is no reply from the Queen Allison or the Queen's spaceship
on Earth.

On the Queen's spaceship the captain has completed his in-
vestigation. He has called every number in his Mars Government
address book. Every phone is answered by a zombie. This is very
infuriating as zombies take so long to answer the phone. First it is
the..HELLO....then it is the...WHAT......DO....YOU....WANT.... The
Mars spaceship captain has fallen asleep five times during his in-

vestigation. Once he even fell off his captain's seat and bumped his head.

The caption goes off to find Queen Allison and tell her the bad news.

◆ ◆ ◆

Step-H is very angry. There is still no reply from Earth. Step-H sends a second email threatening grave consequences that will involve kidnap and tickle torture. Again, there is no reply from Earth. Step-H iso very, very, very angry. She calls her fellow zombies in ZAP to discuss the situation. They decide to send their top Zombie Crack Kidnap Hit Squad to Earth immediately.

◆ ◆ ◆

As the Zombie Hit Squad is preparing to take off, Step-H contacts Dump. She needs to know where to send the hit squad.

Dump says he will try to help but he is still stuck in the toilet. He turns on the huge TV and starts to watch all the news stories about Queen Allison's visit.

Dump sends a message back to Steph-H. He tells her that after the official opening of the Mars Embassy in Mopsworth Queen Allison visited lots of world leaders, including Santa Claus where she left her Christmas present list. Queen Allison is now on holiday on the island of Bali and Dump includes a list of all Queen Allison's activities. He finishes his message by asking Step-H if he can please be rescued. Living in a toilet is not much fun.

◆ ◆ ◆

In the zombie spaceship, the hit squad receive their orders from ZAP. They move into action. There are four members of the hit squad. Speedy, Dancer, Zip and Flash.

Speedy will go to Mopsworth. His task is to arrest Ambassador Murray and take him back to Mars. Zip will go to Lapland to interrogate Santa Claus. ZAP need to know what is on Queen Allison's Christmas list. Dancer will go to the White House to free Dump. Finally, Flash will go to Bali to kidnap Queen Allison from under the noses of Captain Zac and his Space Rangers.

The final instruction from ZAP is that to complete their tasks they must all put on disguises. This is because zombies are six foot tall and have blue skins which will look very suspicious on earth. ZAP has put a party costume box on their spaceship to help them with this.

CHAPTER EIGHTEEN

The zombie spaceship flies into the Earth's atmosphere. They all take the opportunity to chew and old shoe and then wish each other good luck. They will contact ZAP when they have completed their individual tasks so that they can be picked up. The zombie spaceship then drops off the Zombie Hit Squad at their selected locations.

Inside the Mars Embassy in Mopsworth, Murray is sitting by the fire. He is still eating mince pies. So far, he has eaten 3,424 mince pies.

Elicia walks into Murray's office accompanied by the Chicken Special Forces. They immediately take up defensive positions around a big pile of mince pies that are still waiting to be eaten.

'Ambassador Murray, I have a security update for you,' says Elicia.

'Please just call me Murray. I hate it when you call me Ambassador Murray, because it means I have to work,' says Murray in a grumpy voice.

'OK Murray, but I really need to talk to you about Queen Allison's security.'

'Tell me,' says Murray.

'The queen's spaceship has received a message from Mars saying the zombies, calling themselves ZAP have taken over Mars and have locked up all the government workers. They have demanded Queen Allison's return to Mars, or they will send a Zombie Hit Squad to kidnap here,' Elicia explains.

'When did they send this?'

'This morning,' Elicia replies.

'If the zombies have taken over Mars, that explains why I have not received my weekly delivery of Gragg Juice. This is very interesting. What does Queen Allison say?' asks Murray.

'Queen Allison refuses to go home because she is having too much fun.'

'Oh, what shall we do? Murray asks. "Do you think they will really send a Zombie Hit Squad?'

'I think ZAP will do it. So I have instructed Captain Zac to increase security. I have also put my Chicken Special Forces on Yellow

Alert.'

'Yellow alert? Isn't Red Alert the highest,' Murray asks.

'Not here. In Mopsworth, Yellow Alert is the highest,' Elicia replies.

'I understand. What do you want me to do?' Murray asks.

'I think you should contact all the world leaders and explain the situation,' Elicia says.

'Can I have one more mince pie before I make the calls?' Murray asks.

'No, you have eaten too many,' Elicia says and tells her Chicken Special Forces to take all the mince pies back to the kitchen.

Murray is now very grumpy. He gets up and goes to his desk to make his calls.

CHAPTER NINETEEN

Zombie Zip lands in Lapland. He is now walking towards Santa Claus's workshop through the snow. He is very cold and wishes that he had made a different decision with his costume, and that he had a warmer hat. Zip is dressed up as clown. His big shoes make it very difficult to walk through the snow and his red nose keeps falling off.

Zip walks into Santa Claus's workshop. He must find Santa Claus. He picks up a box and starts to walk around pretending to be a worker. The problem is that he is a six-foot clown, and the elves are only 2 foot tall. Santa Claus has also warned the elves to look out for anything out of the ordinary after the call from Murray. A six-foot clown carrying a box is definitely not normal.

The elves grab Zip and pull him to the floor. Zip's red nose falls off. His identity is revealed.

'OH....NO...I...HAVE...BEEN.... CAPTURED,' says Zip.

The elves cheer. They tie Zip up. Then twenty elves surround him. They pick Zip up and sing a Christmas song as they carry him to the store cupboard and lock him up.

Zombie Dancer is outside the gates of the White House. He has decided that most Americans like watching the movies, so he is wearing a superhero costume. Dancer is covered from head to foot in a red skintight suit that covers his face and only leaves space for his eyes and mouth. He is wearing blue boots and has a blue cape. Dancer thinks this is the ideal costume to blend in.

As Dancer stands by the gates, a young boy asks him which super-hero character he is?

Dancer is confused. A question requires him to think. Thinking is very hard for Dancer.

'I...AM...RED,' Dancer replies.

'Red what?' asks the boy.

'I...DON'T...KNOW,' replies Dancer.

Dancer tries to do a small dance to distract the boy, but the boy only laughs.

'A superhero doesn't dance. That is stupid, 'says the boy.

Dancer tries to think again. It is hard. He panics.

'I...AM...RED...ZOMBIE,' says Dancer. He thinks this is clever.

'Red Zombie !!' shouts the boy. 'I have never heard of a superhero called Red Zombie.'

The police officers protecting the White House hear the word zombie and react very fast. They have been told to be on high alert for any zombies after Ambassador Murray's call.

'Where is the zombie?' shouts the police officer.

'There,' says the boy pointing at the tall red lycra man.

Dancer tries to escape, but he is too slow. He is arrested.

Zombie Speedy stands outside the front door of the Mars Embassy in Mopsworth and presses the doorbell. He is dressed as a one of the three kings that go to Bethlehem to carry gifts for the baby Jesus. He thinks this is a fantastic disguise just before Christmas. He even has a great question to ask when they open the front door.

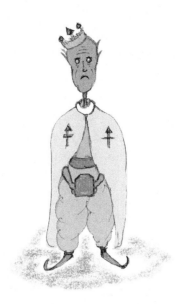

The butler at the Mars Embassy opens the front door. Standing in front of the butler is a tall blue man wearing purple velvet trousers, a red shirt, curly gold shoes, a green cape, a gold crown on top of his bald blue head, and he is carrying a big black box.

'Yes, how can I help you?' says the butler, not put off by the unusual man with the blue head. After working at the Mars Embassy for Murray he has seen many strange things.

'I...AM...LOST....I...AM....LOOKING....FOR....BETHLEHEM....I... COME...IN....YOU...HELP...ME,' says Speedy trying to sound like a king, but failing miserably.

'What is inside the box?' asks the butler.

'STUFF,' replies Speedy.

'What stuff? You cannot come until I know what stuff you have in your box,' replies the butler.

Speedy opens the box and pulls out a ray-gun.

'I....WANT....MURRAY...NOW,' says Speedy, pointing the ray-gun at the butler.

Above Speedy's head, two of the Chicken Special Forces abseil down the side of the building. The chickens wave at the butler to get down. Before the butler can reply, Speedy is hit in the chest by a huge squirt of custard.

The Chicken Special Forces surround Speedy. They are all pointing their custard squirter guns at him. Speedy puts his hands up in surrender. He has failed.

Over in Bali, the last remaining Zombie from the Zombie Hit Squad is getting ready to kidnap Queen Allison. He thinks he is very clever. He has studied the queen's holiday activity agenda and knows that today she is having water skiing lessons. But Zombie Flash has never heard of water skiing, but in the costume box he has found a snow skiing outfit. He thinks that this costume will be just fine. Skiing is skiing.

Flash is on the beach at the location of the water skiing lessons. He finds a small wooden hut with the name "Instructor". Flash ties up the water-skiing instructor and waits on the beach for Queen Allison to arrive.

As Queen Allison approaches with her Space Rangers for security, Captain Zac thinks that something is wrong.

The water-skiing instructor is standing there in a white winter skiing suit, wearing goggles, a wooly bobble hat, holding two ski poles and wearing long skis. Captain Zac then notices that the hands holding the ski poles are blue.

Captain Zac instructs his space rangers to surround the skiing instructor.

'Don't move,' shouts Captain Zac.

Flash realises that his disguise is not working and turns to run. He falls over the long skis and lands in a big heap on the floor. He has also failed.

The Zombie Hit Squad have now all been arrested. They have been locked up in The Tower of London. The Queen of England has told her Beefeaters to make sure that the zombies never escape. She has put Sir Ralph in charge of The Tower of London.

Sir Ralph instructs the Beefeaters to tickle all the zombies until they confirm that there are only four members of the hit squad. After ten hours of tickling and terrible screams of laughter, the Beefeaters have used over thirty tickling sticks. But finally they can confirm that there are only four members of the Zombie Hit Squad.

Back in Mopsworth Elicia reports to Murray that with all the Zombie Hit Squad having been arrested. Queen Allison is now safe. Murray is very happy and tells his chef to serve tea, custard and cake for everyone to celebrate.

Dump sees the news of the Zombie Hit Squad being arrested on the TV in his toilet. He cries. He knows that he will not be rescued today.

Dump sends a message to ZAP telling them that their mission to kidnap Queen Allison has failed.

CHAPTER TWENTY

Steph-H receives the message from Dump about the failure of the Zombie Hit Squad. She knows now that ZAP can only do one thing. They must invade earth. Step-H types out a message for all the leaders of earth.

Dear Leaders of Earth,

We are ZAP, the new leaders of Mars. We have asked Queen Allison very nicely to come back to Mars. She refuses. We sent zombies to bring her back. You have arrested them and put them in The Tower of London. We are very upset now.

We, ZAP, have decided that we will invade earth. We will take control. You will be slaves of Mars and we will make our friend, Ronald Dump the new leader of Earth.

We will invade in five days time.

ZAP, the new rulers of Mars.

Step-H is very happy with her message. She presses send.

She hopes that Murray reads the message as well. She was a food preparation slave in Murray's home for many years on Mars.

Now the power will be on the other green foot, as they say in Greendung. The reason Steph-H is the leader of ZAP is because she became the first ever zombie news reporter on TV after Benjy, Rio and Elicia won the Intergalactic Games. After that the other zombies know that Step-H is special. She is a leader, and she is their idol. The zombies also know that now they can do more things than just being slaves.

CHAPTER
TWENTY ONE

The message from Step-H has been received by all the world leaders. They are all panicking. The politicians are scared. They don't want to lose their jobs.

The other big point about Step-H's message is that they will invade in five days' time. In five days' time it is Christmas Eve. This means that if the zombies succeed and take over the world there will be no Christmas lunch served on Christmas Day, no cracker pulling. And more importantly, children will not be able to open their Christmas presents. Something has to be done!!

The children of the world send messages to all the world leaders, begging them to save Christmas.

◆ ◆ ◆

The world leaders meet at the United Nations building in New York to discuss how they can save the world from a zombie invasion. They are joined by Queen Allison.

There is lots of noise in the General Assembly Hall as all the world leaders try to talk at the same time. Queen Allison bangs her hand on the table for silence.

'Be quiet,' Queen Allison shouts. 'We must all work together.'

'But what can we do,' says the Italian Prime Minister. 'We have no spaceships. We have no way to defend ourselves. What can we do?'

Queen Allison replies. 'The first thing you should know is that the zombies from Mars are very stupid. When they land they will not know what to do. This is our opportunity. We can confuse them. But, this is as long as they don't land all at the same time.'

'What happens if they do that?' asks the President of France.

'Then we are all finished. There will be too many of them,' admits Queen Allison.

'What is the % of probability that they will all land at the same time?' asks the Italian Prime Minister.

'Errrm, maybe 95% to 98%,' replies Queen Allison.

'So there is a high chance that it is all over anyway, whatever defenses we build,' replies the President of France. 'History will repeat, and we will live under occupation again.'

'Then we must stop them from reaching earth in the first place,' says Queen Allison defiantly.

'How?' asks the President of the USA.

'We build spaceships,' says Queen Allison. 'If we cannot build spaceships, we will convert anything we can find into a spaceship. Because we must save Earth and Mars from zombie rule.'

'But we don't have the technology to do that. Guff, Guf, Guwahhh,' says a scruffy man that looks more like a ball, with a blonde tuft of hair on top. He has a silly British accent.

'I will give you the technology. I also met a very clever scientist the other day, a Professor Dan. With my technology and his custard engines we can make hundreds of spaceships. We can also make custard cannons and custard missiles. We will assemble a fleet of spaceships in Mopsworth to save the world. From there we will launch our attack on the zombie spaceships.'

'Can we really do it in five days?' says the Italian Prime Minister.

Queen Allison stands up and bangs her chest. '**Stop being so negative. We need to act together. We shall fight on the beaches, we shall fight on the landing grounds, we shall fight in the fields and in the streets, we shall fight in space. We shall never surrender,**'

There is huge cheer from all the world leaders. For the first time since receiving Step-H's message, they now have hope again and a plan.

Before the meeting breaks up, someone asks what they should do about Dump.

'We need to find the silly man first. Guff, Guf, Guwahhh,' says the round ball with the blonde tuft of hair.

'I think I have an idea of where he is,' says the US President with a smile.

◆ ◆ ◆

Following the meeting at the United nations, extra security staff are put around the White House. It is not for the US President. No, it is to stop Dump escaping. He is now a collaborator with the zombie enemy. Dump is now the most hated man in America and the world.

◆ ◆ ◆

On TV, Dump sees that the Zombie from Mars will invade. He is happy. His new friends will release him soon and make him the next leader of Earth. Dump sends a message to Step-H.

Dear ZAP, we will make Earth and Mars great again. I just know I can help you, because I am the best. Everything I do is great. Your are great. I am great...We are just the greatest.

Your Best Friend

R. Dump,

President of Earth   (I just love the way that
sounds...hehehe)

CHAPTER TWENTY TWO

Earth is on a war footing. Every country is focused on building their home defenses. All soldiers are called back from their Christmas holidays. Lots of homes start to stockpile foods. Christmas puddings in Europe. Hot dogs in the United States. Rice in Asia. Tacos in South America. Sausages in Australia. Dumplings in China. Falafel in the Middle East and Corn in Africa.

In Mopsworth, there is so much activity. Work is split into two areas. Building spaceships and making weapons to fight the zombies.

For weapons, the world leaders have decided that custards cannons, custard squirt guns and custard missiles are the best weapons. They will stop the zombie ships, but they will not hurt the zombies. Queen Allison is very insistent that no zombies must be hurt defending earth. As the weapons will be made with custard, Elicia and Murray have been put in charge of getting them all ready and fixing them to the spaceships.

Building the spaceships is a bigger challenge. Professor Dan is looking at the Mars spaceship technology. The science is amazing.

Professor Dan counts the number of spaceships the earth has. Four old Nasa space shuttles, Captain Zac's spaceship, three spaceships from China, two spaceships from Russia, one spaceship from Europe made from different parts and a few very small spaceships owned by crazy billionaires. The total is fourteen. This is not very many at all. Professor Dan knows that he needs to come up with a solution, and fast.

The first thing that Professor Dan does is to instruct the Mopsworth University and Development Centre stop making custard powered taxis and starts making flying saucers. Taxis and flying saucers are about the same size, so this is logical. But Dan thinks even with the fourteen existing spaceships and five days of flying saucer production they will never have enough spaceships to defeat the zombie spaceship fleet.

Professor Dan puts on this thinking cap. They need to look at this in a different way. Then Professor Dan remembers what Queen Allison told the world leaders. She said that they can convert normal Earth objects into spaceships. Professor Dan smiles and starts writing a list of things he can convert. Once Professor Dan collects all these items, he can start to add custard space engines, a custard cannon and a plastic dome so that the pilot can breathe in space.

Every time Professor Dan adds a new object to convert into a spaceship to his list he laughs. He is going to have a lot of fun converting these things into spaceships.

To help the world fight against the zombies even Benjy and Rio in Bali are helping. They are creating a new custard flavour to be used in the custard weapons. It is called Rendang Fire Custard. It is a spicy custard that if used on the zombies and Dump will turn their skin a bright red colour with yellow spots. The Rendang Fire Custard also makes the skin of any person, or zombie, it hits very, very itchy. It is the perfect anti-zombie weapon.

CHAPTER TWENTY THREE

On Mars, the zombies have amassed 500 spaceships. Each spaceship will carry 10,000 zombies. The zombies have all had breakfast and are ready to go and invade earth. Their leader, Step-H has also told them all to have a bath before they board their spaceships and to give their teeth a good clean. They maybe invading a planet today, but that does not mean personal hygiene is not important.

Step-H will command the lead ship. She will send messages to all the other zombie spaceships from her onboard computer telling them what to do.

The zombies are ready to go. Step-H says they will leave at 1pm. This means that in two hours, half a million zombies will be heading towards earth.

This gives a few zombies at least a couple of hours to look at a map of the universe and work out where Earth is. A few zombies had got lost looking for the bathroom that morning, so going to finding another planet was a big deal.

Back on Earth, things are almost ready. Professor Dan and his team are working twenty-four hours a day to convert as many objects as they can into spaceships from Professor Dan's list. All the spaceships being built are being powered by Mopsworth Custard.

After the spaceships are completed, Elicia, Murray and her Chicken special Forces fix custard missiles, custard squirters and custard cannons to the Earth spaceships.

Queen Allison is very proud of all the work that is going into the preparations. Hovering in front of her and rising high into the sky is Earth's new battle fleet.

The Earth's spaceships are split into three groups. A main spaceship battle group and two squadrons of fighters that will protect the battle group and attack the zombie spaceships.

The Earth's spaceships will be led by Queen Allison's spaceship. On the main deck will be Captain Zac, Queen Allison, Elicia, and Professor Dan. This is quite difficult for Elicia because she is so tall. Captain Zac tells Elicia to sit in the Captain's chair because it has the biggest amount of leg room. Elicia sits down and smiles. She is looking straight at the main screen. She will have the best view of the battle.

On the bridge of the spaceship is a large Christmas tree. It is decorated with lights and tinsel. It is there to remind everyone what they are fighting for.

After the Earth Battle Fleet launches, Captain Zac will take command of the battle fleet.

The main battle group consists of Queen Allison's spaceship, the Earth Space Ranger's spaceship, twenty-eight Mopsworth flying saucers, ten converted old Morris Minor cars, twelve converted London Buses, three converted White Vans, thirty-nine converted submarines, a model of the Millennium Falcon, a model of the Starship Enterprise, a half-built Death Star, and a converted Amusement Pier.

The world's best fighter pilot, Wing Commander Maya will lead the world's first fighter squadron made up of twenty converted bathtubs. The second fighter squadron will be led by Murray using a mixture of unusual spaceships. In his squadron he has red phone boxes, rowing boats, wheelie bins, mobility scooters and lastly Santa Claus on his sleigh with his reindeer. In his sleigh he has a large custard cannon that will be fired by his elves.

All together the Earth Battle Group has one hundred and fifty-seven spaceships.

Captain Zac has been training all the new pilots. He is having an interesting time trying to teach the fighter pilots how to fly tin baths and mobility scooters into space.

It is approaching 12 midday Earth time on Christmas Eve. They must launch now if they are to be on time to meet the Zombie Attack Fleet in space and save Christmas.

The order to launch is given by Captain Zac. All the fighter pilots race to their spaceships. Thousands of earth soldiers are already sitting in the main battle group spaceships.

As Earth's battle group rises into the sky it leaves behind a huge yellow cloud from all the custard engines. It is a beautiful sight.

Captain Zac sends a message to all the spaceships. 'Earth spaceships, we are facing an epic battle to save the earth and save Christmas. Let us be victorious.'

A big cheer is heard from all the spaceships and the small fighters.

Dump is sitting on the presidential toilet, watching TV. He sees the Earth battle group launch. He sends a message to ZAP and tells them that the Earth spaceships are on the way.

Dump is so excited. He thinks that the Earth battle group is no match for the superior zombie attack fleet. Soon he will be president of the world. He writes down what his first act as will be as World President. He smiles. He will make everyone wear one of his favourite baseball caps which will have a picture of his face on it. Maybe one day he can become President of the Universe. He starts to write a new slogan for his baseball caps "Make the Universe Great Again".

CHAPTER TWENTY FOUR

The Earth battle group has been flying for two hours and passes the moon when they see the zombie attack fleet coming towards them. Facing the Earth battle group are hundreds of zombie spaceships.

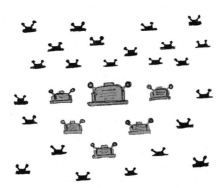

Captain Zac tells Wing Commander Maya to attack the zombies from the left and Murray to attack the zombies from the right. Their job is to fire their custard cannons and custard missiles at the zombie spaceship engines.

Captain Zac then tells all the main battle spaceships to fire their custard cannons at the zombie spaceship windscreens. He hopes that if the windscreens are covered in custard, they will not be able to see where they are going.

The battle is intense. At first, Earth is successful, and they take out ten zombie spaceships. Queen Allison starts dancing around the bridge of her spaceship. She is very happy.

But then the zombies start firing back with their ray-guns. They take out five bathtubs, two mobility scooters, a London bus and damage the Starship Enterprise's engines. All the three white vans are gone.

Captain Zac commands Murray to take his fighter squadron and attack the zombie spaceships from behind. Murray does this and has great success. He takes out the engines of another five zombie spaceships.

Then Captain Zac tells Wing Commander Maya to attack Step-H's spaceship. She swoops across space with two bathtubs supporting her. Step-H's spaceship fires at the three bathtubs.

They take evasive action and use the rubber duck formation. This confuses Step-H's spaceship. Wing Commander Maya is fearless and fires her custard squirter. She scores a direct target and Step-H's spaceship windscreen is covered in custard.

Not far behind Wing Commander Maya is Santa Claus. He has made three runs past the zombie spaceships. His elves are firing their custard cannon non stope. The elves are almost out of custard.

But the zombie spaceships are getting better at firing their ray-guns. The Earth Battle Group spaceships are being hit a lot more times now. Earth is starting to lose the battle.

'What can we do? We are outnumbered,' says Captain Zac.

'Can we send the flying saucers to attack the zombie spaceships from behind?' asks Queen Allison. She has stopped dancing now.

'No, then the main Battle Fleet will be defenseless,' says Captain Zac.

'I have an idea,' says Professor Dan.

'What is it? I hope it is good. Or the battle is lost and so is Christmas,' says Elicia.

'I have been developing a "Custard Computer Virus". It could disable the zombie spaceships. But it is still in development. I don't know if it will work,' says Professor Dan.

'It is our last hope. How do we use it?' says Captain Zac.

'We send Step-H's spaceship a message. It will infect her computer and fill it up with custard. When she sends a message to the other zombie spaceships, it will infect them as well. Then the zombies will not know what is going on. We can then attack and disable all the zombie spaceship engines,' says Professor Dan.

'Let's do it,' says Queen Allison.

'What will the message say?' asks Captain Zac.

'Merry Christmas,' says a smiling Professor Dan.

Professor Dan writes the message and sends it to Step-H's space-ship. Then they wait.

Steph-H receives the message on her computer. At first nothing happens. She continues to send battle commands to all her spaceships.

'KEEP...FIRING...WE...NEED...TO...STOP...THEM,' commands Steph-H.

'WE...ARE...TRYING....BUT...IT...IS...VERY....HARD...TO....HIT... A...BATH TUB...A....SLEIGH,...OR...A...PHONE BOX...WITH...A... RAY-GUN,' replies the weapons officer on her spaceship.

''NO...EXCUSES,' says Step-H.

Then a funny thing happens. Step-H's computer screen starts to fill up with custard and turn yellow. She cannot write or send anymore messages.

Then the computer screens on all the zombie spaceships also start to go yellow as they fill up with custard. Custard then starts leaking out of all the zombie spaceship's control panels. There is panic as all the zombie spaceships start filling up with custard. The zombies cannot communicate with each other anymore. They start to lose the battle. The zombie spaceships retreat to Mars before they drown in custard inside their own ships.

On the deck of Queen Allison's spaceship there is a huge cheer. Professor Dan's custard computer virus is working. The space battle has been won by Earth.

The Earth Battle Fleet follows the zombie spaceships as they fly back to Mars.

◆ ◆ ◆

Dump cannot believe the news he is watching on the TV. The zombie fleet is retreating to Mars. He tries to contact ZAP and the zombie spaceships. Something strange starts happening. His communicator is also infected with custard It starts to leak custard. The President's bathroom fills up with custard and the doors break open under the pressure. Dump washes out on a sea of custard into the Oval office. The US Secret Service are waiting for him. Dump is arrested for treason.

CHAPTER TWENTY FIVE

Earth's Battle Group continues to Mars. Now they have a new ground battle if they want to beat the zombies and win the war. It is on the streets of Greendung, the Capital of Mars.

Earth's Battle Group lands and the soldiers run out and start fighting the zombies. Earth's space soldiers start firing their custard cannons, custard machine guns, and throwing their sticky custard grenades. They are using the Rendang Fire Custard. Within in minutes there are thousands of red coloured zombies with yellow spots wandering aimlessly around Greendung. The zombies start scratching their skin. The itchiness is sending them crazy. The zombies become very confused and start fighting each other. Some of the zombies are so confused, they stop fighting and start chewing an old shoe they can find.

Captain Zac tells the earth's space army to stop firing custard at the zombies. The zombies are doing the work for them. Captain Zac must do something before the zombies destroy themselves completely. But what can he do?

Wing Commander Maya comes up with a cunning plan. She realises that the zombies are tired, itchy and very, very hungry.

'What if we can get all the zombies into one place?' says Wind Commander Maya.

'How can we do that?' asks Queen Allison.

'What is the largest lockable space in Greendung?' asks Wind Commander Maya.

'Greendung Sports Stadium,' replies Queen Allison.

'The zombies are all hungry. If we can find 500,000 bowls of custard. I can fly them into the Greendung Sports Stadium. We tell the zombies there is free custard in the stadium. Then we sit back and wait for them all to go there and eat,' says Wind Commander Maya.

'It might just work, but it could take hours for the zombies to walk there, you know how slow they are,' says Elicia.

'Yes, agreed. But the zombie war will be over,' says Wind Commander Maya.

'I think it is a great plan, and a risk we must take. What flavour custard shall we use?' asks Murray.

'Zombies love eating shoes,' says Queen Allison.

'I think the Football Boot and Grass flavour will work best,' says Professor Dan.

'I agree,' says Queen Allison.

Captain Zac sends a message to Nasa and asks for 500,000 bowls of Dinosaur Tail flavoured Mopsworth custard to be sent to Mars.

A couple of hours later Wing Commander Maya flys the 500,000 bowls of Football Boot and Grass flavoured Mopsworth custard into the Greendung sports stadium. She puts them right in the centre so the zombies cannot miss them.

A general message is sent out across Greendung telling the zombies that there is free Dinosaur Tail custard in the stadium. They all stop fighting and start walking very slowly to find the free custard.

◆ ◆ ◆

Eventually all the zombies are inside the Greendung sports stadium. The doors are locked, and the zombies are trapped.

The voice of Queen comes over the stadium tannoy. 'Surrender or we will send in the tickle police.'

Step-H releases the war is over. They have lost. She stands in the middle of the stadium and raises he arms to ask for silence.

'MY...FELLOW...ZOMBIES...AND...ZAP...WE...HAVE...LOST...
WE...ARE...TIRED...AND...HUNGRY...AND...VERY..ITCHY......
WE...MUST...SURRENDER.

The zombie war is over. Earth is saved, Mars is saved. Christmas is saved.

Queen Allison sends a message for all the mars government staff to be released from the Martian Great Hall. The doors are opened, and they all come out laughing. For the last few days, all they have drunk is Giggle Juice. It will be a few days before they stop laughing, after that they can return to work.

◆ ◆ ◆

To celebrate the end of the Zombie occupation of Mars, Queen Allison throws a huge party in her Royal Palace in

Greendung. For Captain Zac, Elicia, Professor Dan, Wing Commander Maya and all the pilots and soldiers in Earth's Battle Fleet it is there first ever Christmas Party on Mars.

Queen Allison erects a huge Christmas Tree at her palace. Nasa sends Christmas lunch with all the trimmings, thousands of crackers, piles of mince pies, and presents for everyone so that they can all enjoy Christmas Day.

Deep underground in the royal kitchen, Step-H is already washing dishes. Only nine hundred and ninety-nine years, three hundred and sixty-four days to go.

Dump also has a new job. As a punishment for trying to help the zombies he is now the personal toilet cleaner for Queen Allison. Wherever she goes to the toilet, Dump must follow. All Dump has to look forward too is years and years of cleaning up green slime. It is the worst job in the universe.

CHAPTER TWENTY SIX

One month later Elicia, Captain Zac, Professor Dan, Wing Commander Maya and Murray are Earth's hero's. Their pictures are on the front of every newspaper and magazine. There are memes, Gif's and videos of them all across the internet on Earth and Mars.

Queen Allison starts her second holiday in Bali. This time she does not give her staff the day off. She has learnt her lesson. There will be no zombie invasion when she is away this time.

Today she has invited Elicia, Captain Zac, Professor Dan, Wing Commander Maya, and Murray for lunch to celebrate freedom. Queen Allison has chosen her favourite restaurant in Bali. It is the Custard Beach Cafe. The Cafe is owned by her best friends, Benjy, and Rio. The lunch goes on for many hours. The dish of the day is Grilled Fish served with Lemon flavoured Mopsworth Custard.

It is great to be with friends. They eat and eat until they are so full they can burst. They laugh so hard that their faces start to hurt, and they lose their voices.

It is the best lunch ever.

THE END

ABOUT THE AUTHOR

Alastair Macdonald

Alastair has been reading from an early page and was always encouraged by his parents to read. Reading became a passion and it has always enriched his life.

Alastair has written a variety of novels, ranging from childrens books, to murder mystery novels.

Apart from writing, Alastair is an ultra runner and triathlete.

Printed in Great Britain
by Amazon